Beyond the Golden Hills

Beyond the Golden Hills

and other stories

Anne L. Squire-Buresh

HERALD PRESS
Scottdale, Pennsylvania
Waterloo, Ontario

Library of Congress Cataloging-in-Publication Data
Squire-Buresh, Anne L., 1951-
Beyond the Golden Hills and other stories /
Anne L. Squire-Buresh.
p. cm.
ISBN 0-8361-3547-4
I. Title.
PS3569.Q454B49 1991
813'.54—dc20 90-25891
CIP

The paper used in this publication is recycled and meets the minimum requirements of American National Standard for Information Sciences—Permanence of Paper for Printed Library Materials, ANSI Z39.48-1984.

BEYOND THE GOLDEN HILLS

Published by Herald Press, Scottdale, Pa. 15683
Published simultaneously in Canada by Herald Press,
Waterloo, Ont. N2L 6H7.
Library of Congress Catalog Number: 90-25891
International Standard Book Number: 0-8361-3547-4
Printed in the United States of America
Book and Cover Design by Merrill R. Miller

1 2 3 4 5 6 7 8 9 10 97 96 95 94 93 92 91

This book is dedicated to my family and friends, whose love has sustained and encouraged me.

Contents

Author's Preface

I cannot remember a time when stories and storytelling did not fill me with wonder. My parents told me stories of where their people came from, how they came to America, and the events that shaped them. My favorite family possession is an old album of photographs, some dating back a hundred years. Nearly every person captured on film had a story, a place in the history of my family's past.

Through high school and college, I found an outlet for my pursuit of stories and storytelling: theater. I never got over the sense of wonder and accomplishment when the audience was drawn into the story played out in front of them. The summers I spent in the Champlain Shakespeare Festival in Burlington, Vermont, led me to discover William Shakespeare, one of the world's best storytellers.

Later I discovered what others have found before me: the power and truth of the parables of Jesus. He surely understood that people, even those living in times and places unheard of, could grasp the point of a parable far more easily than a sermon.

We call our stories by many names: parable, allegory, myth, fable, legend, oral tradition, folk tales, and the like. Often the boundary between what is or was real and the cause and effect of that reality finds its voice in story. Stories provide answers that events by themselves cannot answer.

The stories in this book are tales of what could be, or might have been, or even what may occur again and again. Their truth lies, hopefully, in the common thread of everyday life. They are written to be a mirror in which we see in simple, daily choices the possibility of changed lives.

—Anne L. Squire-Buresh
Millbury, Massachussetts

Beyond the Golden Hills

The King's Visit

nce there was a great and mighty king. While still a young man, he had led his mighty army in many battles. By the power of his army, he had conquered all the surrounding nations, and had become their king as well.

This king was so powerful that whatever he asked for, whether great or small, was brought to him at once. His subjects feared him, and the power that comes from mighty armies and great wealth.

But the king grew lonely. He was tired of the political advisers, the slavish courtiers, and the beautiful lords and ladies that waited on his every word. Because everyone seemed to be afraid of him, he no longer knew anyone he could trust as a friend. He wondered if all the people in all his kingdoms were like the flatterers who surrounded him.

So he sent several trusted messengers to the towns and cities of his countries. They were to find a town or city where he could visit and speak to his people, a town where he could learn what it felt like to have real friends.

At last one town was chosen as suitable for the king to visit. In secrecy, but with great excitement, the townspeople prepared for their king's arrival. A few days before his visit, the king sent his most trusted servant to see that all things were ready.

The king's servant found a town full of people cleaning and polishing their homes. Everyone, it seemed, was preparing wonderful gifts to impress the king.

The first home the servant visited was the mayor's household.

"Look how my house shines with beauty. I have marble floors in every room. I have the finest crystal and silver that money can buy. This is the finest home in the land—if not in all the lands the king owns. Look at these gold trimmings on the eaves. They were made by hand. Nothing is too good for the king!" the mayor boasted.

The trusted servant made notes in the little notebook he carried. But he said nothing.

The mayor went on.

"Why, when the king visits my house, he will think he is still at the palace. He will not have to lift a finger to ask for anything. My household and I will see that he lacks nothing."

The servant thanked the mayor. Then he went to the priest's home.

The priest took him to the great cathedral standing in the center of town.

"This is the grandest cathedral in the land, if not the world. I'm sure the king will be proud to be seen worshiping in such a fine cathedral. When the townspeople heard the king was coming, they flocked to the church and gladly poured out their contributions. We built a new altar, made of the finest wood and gilded with gold from the farthest country. Nothing is too good for our king."

Again the trusted servant smiled but said nothing. He just made a note in his book.

The servant of the king went to every home in the town. The goldsmith had made a crown of the finest gold, set with precious stones. The carpenter had made a beautiful throne, inlaid with mother-of-pearl. The tailors and seamstresses were making a magnificent robe of silk and gold braid, all made with wondrous embroidery.

At the end of his visit the trusted servant returned to the mayor. He opened his notebook. After consulting several pages, he turned to the mayor.

"All does seem to be ready," he said. "I wonder, though—of all the towns I have seen, yours is the only one with no poor people, no beggars at your gates. Have you no needy people in your town? Or is there some place, some home I have missed?"

The mayor looked pleased at the question.

"We did have some poor—not many, of course. As for what became of them . . . if you look in the center of town, you'll see a great house that once belonged to a certain woman. Many people thought the women should not be allowed to live here because of her reputation.

"But when she moved here, she kept to herself. We were not about to call on her, but she did not seem to expect us to welcome her anyway.

"But then one day—can you imagine?—she invited

the beggar who used to sit in the town square into her home. The next day she took in the crippled boy his parents were ashamed to look at. The next thing you know, she had a dozen of such people with her.

"Then we heard that the king was coming here. We asked her to please take her little group somewhere else, so they wouldn't make the town look bad.

"So she sold her house in town and moved to an old farm on the edge of town."

After the mayor's speech, the king's servant made a few notes.

Then he said, "Since I have to visit all the homes, I must visit hers as well. Then a decision will be made in a few days about which day the king will visit."

The trusted servant shut his book. He bid the Mayor good-bye, and set out on the road to the edge of town.

As the king's servant rounded the bend in the road, he saw an old stone farmhouse. A young girl in a wheelchair was cheering two small boys as they played with a ball in the dirt road.

The ball sailed though the air and landed at the servant's feet. With a smile, he rolled it back to the boys. The girl applauded him.

"Our mother's in the house, if you're looking for her," the taller of the boys volunteered.

Thanking them, he knocked on the door of the house.

"Come in," a gentle voice called. A woman of indefinite age sat at a table in the neat but bare room, feeding a tiny baby. Her warm brown eyes were all that was left of what must have been great beauty.

At the far end of the room, an old man and woman sat in equally ancient rocking chairs. Two small, shabbily dressed children were setting the table for a meal. The servant noticed that the bowls and plates were old and didn't match. The silverware was battered.

The woman at the table spoke.

"Can I help you?"

The servant of the king explained his mission.

"Are all these people part of your family?" he asked.

"These are the family I have chosen: my parents, my sisters and brothers, my children." With a wave of her hand, she included the children, the old people, and seemingly all the people and creatures outside and in.

As he was about to continue his explanation, the woman put up her hand to stop him. She smiled at him as she put the sleeping baby into a cradle which had been broken and mended.

"It is time for our evening meal. We would be honored if you could join us," she said.

The king's servant realized that the day was almost gone and he was indeed hungry. As he accepted her invitation, he realized that in all the grand and beautiful houses he had visited that day, no one had even offered him a cup of water.

The other children came in from the yard, along with the old woman who had been hanging the wash. The servant joined them as they said a prayer of thanksgiving for their simple meal of soup and bread.

When the meal was ended, the children asked him questions about the king's visit.

The woman said to the king's servant, "We know

why you have come. We know the great king longs to see how his people live—and we hope to have a glimpse of him as he passes through the village. We have no rich gifts to offer him, for we are the humblest of his people."

"How is it that you have this house so far from town?" the servant asked, although he knew part of the story from the mayor.

The woman and all those at the table smiled.

"Long years ago, I was a beautiful and proud woman," she began. "Many men bought me jewels and fine clothes. I was their toy, their decorated doll.

"One day, after a feast at my fine mansion, I noticed that there were poor people at my gate waiting for the scraps from my table. Yet of all the people at the feast, I alone noticed them.

"After that I found myself noticing the ragged beggars in the streets, and the abandoned children, and yes, even the birds with broken wings.

"It no longer seemed right that I had so much wealth and jewels simply because men thought me beautiful.

"So I sold my mansions and my jewels and moved to this village. There I found these friends in need of what I could provide."

"But the people were not kind to us in the village. They would turn away when they saw us coming near them," one of the boys said.

"They liked us even less when they found out the king was coming," said the other boy.

The woman smiled and shrugged. "It seemed easier

to live out here than to live in the midst of people who saw us as animals or less."

"But you will not see the king when he comes to the village," said the servant.

The woman paused for a moment and looked around the table at the faces there. Around the table were the old and the young, those with eyes full of ravages of pain, those with lined faces, and those with the flush of youth.

"There was a time when it was important to me that kings were welcomed and no expense be spared to create gifts and wonders for that king. But that time is long past. I have no regrets at the choice I made to give what I had—even if it means I can offer the king nothing but the hospitality of this home."

The servant wrote in his notebook for a long time.

Then he said, "I must return and tell the king all the things I have seen today."

The woman smiled. "Go in peace. And if you ever come this way again, our door is always open. There will always be a place for you at our table."

As he walked back down the road, the king's most trusted servant looked back. He saw the woman and the children and the old ones waving at him as though in a final blessing.

And when the king came, the people of the town did not see him. Not the mayor. Not the priest. Not the goldsmith. Not the carpenter. Not the tailor.

When the king came to the village, he visited only the humblest of his subjects. It was said that the king and his most trusted servant stayed for many days with the woman and her family.

Often it is still rumored that when the king longs to be with his people again, he comes with his trusted servant to that special place. There the door is always open. The bowls do not match and the spoons are battered, but there is always a place at the table.

The Innkeeper

nce, in the middle of a storm, a weary traveler knocked on the door of an old inn. It was long into night, long past the time when most travelers would have found refuge from the storm and the dark.

After a long time, the door of the inn was opened by a plump, middle-aged man rubbing sleep from his eyes.

A traveler, gray with fatigue and wet from the storm, stood at the door.

"Yes?" the innkeeper asked.

"Have you any rooms left? I have traveled a great distance. My horse went lame and the storm has made further travel impossible."

"No rooms left," the innkeeper said.

"What about your animal shed?" the traveler asked, near to tears. "It's not just for me, you understand, but for my boy."

The traveler tipped back his cloak to reveal a child sleeping in his arms.

"No, not with my animals, either." The traveler feared the innkeeper would close the door. Instead, the innkeeper threw the door open.

"Come in! Come in! I have been expecting you!" the innkeeper smiled in welcome.

The traveler was startled by this warmth. But he took the innkeeper at his word and entered the inn.

"Come, I will show you to my room. After all, you have a greater need than I do." And indeed, the innkeeper showed the traveler to his own room, where the rumpled bedclothes showed how hastily he had risen.

With a word of gratitude, the traveler laid his young son on the bed and covered him. The child never woke but smiled in his sleep at the warmth and comfort of the bed.

"You must be hungry after your journey. Come and I will make you some supper." The innkeeper bustled from the room.

"Surely all your staff are asleep," the traveler said. "I do not want to trouble you any further. The bed for my son was enough."

"No trouble at all. It hasn't been that long since I cooked all the food served here." The innkeeper pulled his guest into the kitchen.

The traveler was glad to have a place to sit. The kitchen was still warm from the supper fire. It was filled with the welcoming aroma of spices and fresh bread.

The innkeeper bustled about. He piled logs on the fire, filled a kettle to hang over the hearth, looked in the pantry for bread and cheese.

For many minutes neither of them spoke. When the

water boiled, the innkeeper made his guest tea, and sat with him as the man eagerly ate his supper.

At last, when the meal was done, the traveler looked curiously at the innkeeper.

"It is very generous of you to give up your bed for us," said the traveler. "Do you offer your bed to all those who come this late when you are full?"

The innkeeper smiled.

"It doesn't matter for one night. I often used to stay up until morning, or sleep in one of the chairs in the great room," the innkeeper said. "As for giving up my bed for a traveler, in truth, I have only done it once before."

As weary as the traveler was, he seemed reluctant to leave the warmth and companionship of the kitchen.

The innkeeper went on. "It was a night almost as stormy as this one, but in midwinter, years and years ago. I don't remember now why the town was so full of travelers, but my inn and everyone else's were full. It was near the middle of the night, but I remember that I hadn't been to bed yet, with all the extra people to prepare meals for."

The innkeeper paused, and smiled to himself at the memory.

"They were so very young, or so they seemed to me, although the man was probably my age then. The woman was so beautiful, I have never seen any woman more lovely, and I have traveled widely."

Again the innkeeper paused.

The traveler urged him on. "What then?"

The innkeeper seemed to come back from his

faraway thoughts. "Oh, yes. I didn't realize until she came inside that she was expecting a child." The innkeeper shook his head and smiled to himself. "I've been widowed now for nearly 10 years, and have grandchildren the age of your son. But back then I knew nothing about children at all.

"They came in, pinched from the cold, for they had traveled a long way that day, especially for a woman close to her time. She had her baby that night, in my bed, in my inn."

The wonder in his voice was still fresh despite the long years. "A beautiful baby, so tiny, yet so perfect. I have kept the image of that beautiful mother and her infant son in my mind ever since.

"It's strange, isn't it?" the innkeeper asked the traveler. "In the years since I have seen many births and more than a few deaths, but that birth is as vivid to me now as though it happened tonight."

In the silence that followed, the innkeeper seemed to have forgotten his guest.

The traveler broke the silence. "What became of them?"

The innkeeper returned to the present with a start. "Oh, after a few days, they continued on their journey. When they left, the woman put her tiny infant son into my arms. Then she smiled at me, and said a blessing for me and for my household. The man, too, said a blessing for me.

"We stood in the courtyard for a long time, it seemed, me with this tiny baby in my arms, and his parents blessing me."

The traveler drank the last of his tea. Suddenly he was aware of great fatigue.

"Here we are chatting on and on, and you are so tired. Please forgive me." The innkeeper was contrite.

"Oh, no," said the traveler, "Your story was glorious. It was only just now that I remembered how long my day has been. I wonder—did you ever see them again?"

"No," said the innkeeper, "for they were from a far country, and their path has never led back here. But the blessing they gave me there in the courtyard has surely been answered.

"It's not that I haven't had times of pain, you understand, but that I have never had a moment since that day that I have felt alone. It's as though they have never left me, as though somehow, by some great power, they have become a part of my life. Odd, isn't it?

"You see," he continued, "at the time I let them use my room it didn't matter to me, it wasn't a very big thing to do at all. And such wonder and blessing came from it. Now I would be willing to sleep with my animals outside every night to see that wonder and joy once again."

"But come, you must be exhausted," and the innkeeper led the traveler to his own room.

The next morning, as the traveler and his son were continuing on their journey, he stopped in the courtyard with the innkeeper. The little boy smiled up at the innkeeper and slipped his small hand into the innkeeper's large one. The little boy's father leaned over and whispered in the boy's ear.

The boy smiled a shy smile. "We ask blessings on you and your house, now and forever."

The innkeeper's heart was filled with the sudden warmth of great joy. He leaned over and touched the boy's cheek with his free hand. "And peace go with you, now and forever."

The innkeeper watched as the traveler and his son walked away from the inn. The rising sun poured out its warm splendor on the courtyard. It was a beautiful morning.

The Sandcastle

n a small town, there once lived a man whose wife died after many years of marriage. The man was heart-broken. Even the presence of his sons and daughters and his grandchildren did not seem to heal the awful emptiness in his heart.

Finally he resolved to kill himself. Since he lived near the shore of the great ocean, he decided to drown himself.

Early one morning he set off down the shoreline of the ocean, trying to get up the courage to walk into the sea forever. His walk took him past a young girl making a sandcastle at the edge of the sea.

Not wanting to talk to her or anyone, he turned to walk back the way he came. But she stopped him.

"Please, sir, could you help me?" her young voice called to him.

The man shook his head as he walked faster away from her.

But her voice stopped him again.

"Please, sir—" she began again.

The man turned, angered at the interruption.

"No! I cannot help you. Now stop bothering me!"

Even as he barked the harsh words, he walked rapidly back down the shore.

He spent the whole day walking farther and farther down the beach. The tide was coming in when he finally turned and walked back up the miles of shore. As he passed the spot where the little girl had been in the morning, he saw the remnants of her sandcastle being washed away by the incoming tide.

The man shook his head at the futility of her efforts. As he watched the water rush over the last bit of the castle wall, he realized the daylight was fading. He had not been able to walk into the sea.

After another bitter night of loss and anger, the man made up his mind that this day he would indeed kill himself. But as he walked down the shore, he saw the girl beginning to build a new sandcastle.

Before she could say a word, he spoke sternly.

"Build it further away from the water's edge or the tide will wash it away again."

Without waiting for a reply he walked past her up the shoreline. Again, he was alone with his thoughts for the whole day, until the tide began to turn.

As he walked slowly back to his empty house, he walked by the sandcastle the girl had made. She had made it farther away from the water's edge. The incoming tide had not touched it. But the walls, weak and unshapely, had not survived the day.

Despite another sleepless night, he was curious to know if the girl would return to the shore. Instead of beginning his long walk down the shoreline, he decided to start where the girl had been. Indeed she was there before him.

As he walked past her, he said, "Take wet sand, and shape it with a board, and your walls will stand longer."

Although she said nothing, her smile was her reward.

For the third day, he walked for miles and miles down the lonely shore, with only the waves and the gulls as company for his black thoughts.

When he turned back this time, the tide was high. He wondered if the girl had done as he suggested.

As he walked by the sandcastle, he found that the tide had not washed it away. The walls had been shaped by a board and the wet sand made them sturdy. But still, it was not a very good sandcastle, lacking symmetry and grace.

That night, for the first time in many days, he was able to sleep a little. Still, he was awake long before dawn. As he lay in the darkness, he remembered that his children, now grown, once had small pails and shovels they used to make sandcastles.

For a long time, he debated with himself whether to take the effort to find them, and why it even mattered to him. At last he decided to look for the pails and shovels.

As he searched the trunk in the attic, he came across letters he had written long ago to his wife. It was still too dark to read them in the attic, so he took the letters and the pails and shovels with him.

When he came to the shore, the castle, attacked all

night by wind and tossed spray, was nearly gone. The girl was nowhere in sight, so he put the pails and shovels on the pile of sand.

That day, as he walked down the shore, he read the packet of letters. Long ago, before marrying, he had gone away to find work in a distant city. But he had written to his wife-to-be nearly every day, filling page after page with events and people he had met.

Each letter was filled with the tenderest words of love and hope. He could remember those months of work so long ago now, but the words he had written had long slipped from his memory.

As he read the letters, tears poured from his eyes and blurred the words on the page. Finally he found he no longer had the strength to walk. He sat on an outcropping of rock and cried for his loss.

It was only when the tide began to turn that he recalled where he was. The long and sleepless nights had begun to take their toll. He longed to be home.

Again he walked past the place where the girl had made her sandcastle. She had put the pails and shovels to good use. The walls were tall and shapely, the structure firm and graceful. The pails and shovels lay at one side of the castle. He left them there, for he had no desire to return them to the attic chest.

That night, he slept the whole night through. In the morning, he found he was hungry for the first time in many, many days.

Although the day was gray and overcast, he decided to walk down the shore and see if the girl would be out building her castle.

She was there, despite the growing chill in the air and the white-capped waves. As he approached, she looked up with an expression of doubt on her face.

"I've come to see if you still needed any help," he said.

"Oh, yes! Today I am going to build the best sandcastle yet." Her smile was infectious. He found himself smiling ever so slightly in return.

She went on.

"I want to build it up with stones and shells so it won't wash away at all."

The man nodded. It had been a long time since he had spent time with a child, and a much longer time since he had built a sandcastle. It had also been a long time since he had laughed or even smiled at anything or anyone.

"I'll go and find stones and shells for the walls," he said, "if you want to start on the walls."

"Can we have a moat, too? And towers? I don't know how to make them, but I saw them once in a picture." The girl laughed in anticipation.

"Oh, yes, a moat and towers, of course. And maybe a dragon outside the moat." His voice nearly cracked on the mix of sorrow and peace that her words brought to his troubled heart.

As he looked for flat stones and shells for the walls, the girl began digging out the moat and clearing a space for the great castle they would build.

And build they did! They spent all the day working on the castle. By the time they finished, the tide was coming in, ragged and wind-whipped.

But their castle was magnificent. It boasted a great wide moat, eight tall towers walled with stone, gardens of sea-seed, terraces, stairs, double-walls with a walkway along the top edge. It even had a dragon inlaid with tiny shells lying outside the moat. It was truly a sandcastle above all sandcastles.

"Tomorrow?" the girl asked the man shyly as they dusted the sand off their hands.

He nodded, hoping she would not take it for a promise.

That night a great storm lashed the sea and shore. The thunder and lightning was the worst ever seen in that area. The sea roared with a life of its own.

The storm blew itself out by morning. The dawn came clear and warm, and doubly welcome after such a night of violence.

The man was the first one to the shore. The storm had destroyed the sandcastle. Nothing remained—not one stone, shell, weed, wall, nor moat. The man was filled with anger and pain.

When the girl arrived, she looked at the destruction with deep sadness.

"That's it, then," the man said, his voice bitter with tears.

"What do you mean?" she asked him, her own voice choking.

"It's gone, destroyed—we can never make it over the same way. What does it matter, anyway?" He turned so she would not see his anger and rage.

But she touched his hand softly.

"You mean that you don't want to build another

one? Weren't you happy when we built the sandcastle yesterday?" She seemed puzzled.

He turned back to her.

"Yes," he admitted slowly.

"And when we were done, were you happy with what we had made?"

"Yes," he admitted. "It was the finest sandcastle I have ever seen." He smiled at the memory.

"It was the very best I have ever seen, too. And I would never have been able to build it without you. That's what I'm telling you. We built something together that was the very best. Even if the storm destroyed the sandcastle, we still had the very best.

"If we don't build another, the sea will think it won, don't you see?" Her earnest face, with her eyes full of wonder and joy, looked into his.

But he was not consoled.

"Why bother making another when the sea will only wash it away again?"

Her face clouded.

"Because it seems like the best thing to do. And I want to build another one. I want this one to have ten towers and two dragons. Do you want to help?"

For a moment he was lost in thought. He wanted to help. But he knew that even another sandcastle more beautiful than the first could never last.

With a great sigh, he spoke.

"I do want to help you. But I think I'll go and get some people who are really good at sandcastles. I have grandchildren who haven't seen me for weeks. I know that together you and I and they will make the very best sandcastle the world has ever seen."

He smiled at her and felt the warmth of the sun on his face. Overhead, the gulls whirled in their endless dance. And beyond him, the sea glistened with endless life.

The Stableboy

n a small country, there once lived a very rich man. As he had been born into a family which owned great tracts of land, he enjoyed all the privileges great wealth and political power can bring. His greatest joy was that he owned the finest stable of riding horses in the land.

This wealthy man had a vast army of servants. They ranged from well-educated and well-spoken house servants down to poor field and stable hands.

Most of the house servants lived on the rich man's grounds in small cottages. The poorer field and stable workers lived in a collection of tumble-down shanties outside the manor's lands, down by the river's edge.

One young boy from the shantytown worked as the rich man's stableboy. He did the rough work for the rich man's grooms—cleaning stables, polishing harnesses and, on occasion, holding the horses for the rich man and his friends to mount.

One morning, the rich man and his closest friend and adviser, the mayor of the village, prepared to go riding. As was the rich man's custom, he tossed a small coin to the stableboy who held the horses. But that morning, the boy who caught the coin spoke to the rich man.

"Thank you, sir, but I would rather have the apple you are about to feed your horse." Although the stableboy's voice was soft, the audacity of his request was like a shout.

The rich man was as surprised at the boy's words as he would have been if his horse had suddenly spoken. The mayor began to scold the boy in a loud tone. But the rich man silenced his friend with a sudden gesture. Then he looked closely at the boy for a long moment.

"Keep the coin. Go and take an empty grain bag. Pick as many apples as you like from the trees in the orchard."

With that the rich man and his friend wheeled their horses and rode off.

The next morning, as the rich man prepared to go riding, the same stableboy held his horse.

"And how did you like my apples, boy?" he said to the boy.

"I did not eat any of them." The boy replied in his soft voice.

"None? What happened to them?" The rich man was surprised.

"I gave them to my mother and my friends. They had never tasted apples before. There were no apples left for me." The simplicity of the boy's voice touched the rich man.

"Then take another bag of apples with you today." Again the rich man tossed a coin to his stableboy and left.

The day after this, the rich man was visiting the stables to inspect his new stallion. He saw the boy cleaning the leather bridles and stopped to speak to him.

"Well, lad, did you taste my apples this time?"

The boy shook his head.

For a moment, it seemed as though the rich man would become angry at the boy. In truth, the rich man had often been angry with far less reason.

"Take a third bag home, and be sure you eat one." The rich man turned back to the more pressing issues of his horses.

The next day, as the rich man mounted his horse for his morning ride, the boy again stood at the horse's head, holding the reins.

"Well? Did you have one of those apples?"

"Yes." From beneath his ragged coat, the boy drew out a piece of folded paper. "I was told to give you this."

The rich man took the paper. Unfolding it, he read a simple note. "Dear Sir, Thank you for your apples."

It was signed by three people.

In all his life, no one had ever thanked the rich man unless they had to. Surprisingly moved, he put the letter in his pocket.

"How long have you worked for me, boy?" he asked the stableboy.

"Two months, sir."

"And how much are you paid?" The rich man knew it could not be much, for the stableboy was one of the lowest of his servants.

"Four coins a week, sir," came the quiet reply.

"And what do you do with this fortune?" To the rich man, it did not seem enough to buy even the smallest meal.

The boy answered simply.

"I buy food for my mother. I am saving what is left over to buy her a blanket, for she is so very cold at night."

From his seat on the great horse, the rich man could see his vast holdings of land, his beautiful, many-roomed mansion, his lands under cultivation, his great barns where his horses were well cared for.

He could also see the boy, in his ragged clothes, his thin, pale face, and his large dark eyes. But he only wheeled his horse around and left the stableboy watching him from the barn.

That night, a fire started in one of the cottages. How it happened, no one was ever sure. But within a short time it had spread through the old cottages by the river. The blaze could be seen as far as the manor house where the rich man lived.

By the time his servants told the rich man about the fire, it had already consumed most of the cottages. The rich man immediately called for his fastest horse and he leaped on it without a coat or hat.

Even riding at a gallop, it seemed like eternity until the rich man reached the cottages. They were now completely swallowed up by fire.

The rich man jumped from his panting horse. He flung the reins at one of the children standing at a distance from the blaze.

For a few desperate moments he scanned the crowd

for some sign of the stableboy. When he saw him, the rich man was filled with greater relief than he had ever experienced.

The boy, covered with the soot of the fire, saw the rich man as well. After a brief pause, the boy walked to where the rich man stood.

"I knew you would come, sir." The boy said.

"How could you know? I only knew myself a few moments ago that I was coming." But even as he spoke, the rich man found himself wanting only to know if the child was all right.

In time, the fire burned itself out, leaving behind only a few charred timbers. Many of the people in the crowd were weeping openly.

The man turned to the boy.

"Where will these people go now that they have no homes?"

The boy did not answer for a long time.

"They will sleep here until tomorrow, then most will go to live with other friends or family."

"Would they stay here if their homes were rebuilt?" the rich man asked.

"This is our home," the boy answered simply.

"Wait here. I'll be back as soon as I can." The man mounted his horse and rode away.

Before dawn, he returned with three wagons. The crowd of families still stood among their ruined homes, tears on their faces, staring at the charred rubble.

"My friends," the rich man began, "you are welcome to stay on my land until your homes are rebuilt. That is, if you want to stay. I have many tents that you may use, and my kitchen will feed you."

A murmur went through the tired, soot- and tear-streaked crowd of families. One man, holding a tiny child in his arms, spoke up.

"Why are you doing this? What do you want in return?"

At the man's blunt question, a murmur ran through the crowd.

The rich man, sitting on his horse, said nothing for a time, then commented, "I want nothing in return. If you want to come with me, my wagons will take you." As though he had said too much, the rich man wheeled his horse and left them standing there.

Most, although not all, of the people accepted the offer. A tent city sprang up outside the stable, and the rich man's kitchen staff brought the people food.

By the afternoon after the fire, the news of the rich man's guests had spread to the village beyond the manor. The rich man's friend, the mayor, came to check out the rumors. He seemed surprised at the rich man's generosity.

"This is quite a new thing for you, isn't it? Though what you want to do with these people is beyond me." The mayor's mocking tone did not seem to touch the rich man, who had been standing at the great window in his study when the mayor entered.

Suddenly, with long strides, the rich man stood in front of the mayor. With a voice that more than hinted of anger, the rich man spoke. "You will not speak of my friends that way—not today, not ever."

The mayor was startled. "These people are your friends?"

"Friends? Did I call them friends? No, they aren't my friends."

As the rich man paused, the mayor interrupted.

"For a moment I thought you had lost your senses."

But the rich man went on as though the mayor had not spoken.

"From now on, these people are my family, my people. You and I, my friend, are going to see that they realize it. If they need jobs, you and I will see they find jobs. If they are in need of food or clothes or schools or doctors, you and I will help them get what they need. Do you understand?"

By the end of the speech, the rich man stood directly in front of the mayor.

"But why are you doing this?" The Mayor unknowingly echoed the man from the crowd.

Again the rich man did not answer.

The mayor spoke again.

"They won't thank you, you know. And you'll probably go bankrupt if you really do these things."

There was a discreet knock on the study door. One of the man's servants came in.

"Excuse me, sir, but there is a boy from the stable asking to see you. I told him you would not see him."

The rich man shook his head.

"Show him in. And from now on, if any of the people from the cottages ask to speak with me, you are to let them in."

The servant looked puzzled. But then, with a nod,

the servant turned and brought the stableboy into the rich man's study.

For a few moments the boy stood looking about him at the great tiers of books, the beautiful furnishings, and the wonderful tall windows. Finally, the boy recalled his errand.

"I came to thank you, sir, and my neighbors also thank you."

After another long moment of silence, the rich man spoke softly to the boy.

"You have worked for me for several months. I have seen you every day, and yet I do not even know your name."

The boy smiled.

"My name is Timothy, sir."

The rich man smiled in response.

"And my name is not sir. It is Michael. I am very pleased to know you. Now, come and introduce me to your neighbors. We have much work to do together."

At the door, the rich man stopped and turned back to the mayor.

"As for why I'm doing this—I don't really know myself. But wouldn't you help your brother or your sister or their children if you could?"

After a pause, the rich man added, "Are you coming?"

With a final questioning look on his face, the mayor said, "I think you are crazy. But you have been my friend for 40 years. We might as well be crazy together. Of course I'm coming with you. Just let me get my hat."

Beyond the Golden Hills

Once there was a band of pilgrims who had traveled from a far country. Their long and perilous journey took them over steep mountains, through harsh scrub lands set with brambles, and into a bleak and barren desert. But they endured all these things because they searched for the wondrous land beyond the golden hills.

This land was said to be the most beautiful of any land, anywhere in the world. It was said to be a land of great wonders, where the air itself caressed the ear with the song of celestial choirs, where the waters were always sweet and clear, where all who came lived in harmony, peace, and thankfulness.

The route to this land was dotted with the abandoned tents of pilgrims who had turned back. More ominous, though, were the stone markers of those who had died on the journey.

But this group of pilgrims was determined to find the land beyond the golden hills. They had already endured the cold and bitter climb through the high mountain pass. They had struggled through the wilderness where the path was lost in the dense brambles that tore at their skin.

At last they came to the vast arid plain that was the last obstacle before the golden hills. The group had hoped they could cross the desert in a few days, but they had already spent weeks on the crossing. The hills had looked deceptively close, and even after weeks, they still seemed just beyond the reach of their hands.

Finally, after several more weeks of travel in the endless desert, they had exhausted their food and their water. Their leader, whose exhausted face made him appear far older than his years, gathered them at evening.

"I will go out with scouts in the morning to see if we can reach the hills in another day. If we cannot, then all hope of reaching the golden land beyond the hills is lost," he said.

They slept restlessly that night, huddled together to gain a little precious warmth, for the nights were very cold in the desert.

In the morning, the leader walked with the scouts to the next rise. As they came to the top of the rise, a magnificent sight met their eyes. Before them was a splendid oasis, with bright silk tents rippling in the breeze. A pool of clear water shone in the middle of a grove of trees.

At first they did not trust their eyes, for travelers had often told them tales of the mirages that came with exhaustion and hunger. But as the leader and the scouts approached, it grew larger and more real with each step.

While they were still a long way off, a man came running toward them. Even at a distance they could see he was ancient and lined. But his welcome was as warm and delighted as a child's.

"Welcome, strangers! Welcome! Are there more of you? Come to my station and rest. Come!" And he pulled them toward his tents.

The leader spoke. "I must go and get the others for we are indeed tired and hungry." The leader ran quickly back. In minutes the whole group of exhausted, hungry travelers stood in the midst of the oasis.

They looked around them in wonder, for truly this was a wonderful sight. There were baths of copper with fires underneath, ready to heat the water from the spring. There were soft towels and fine garments to wear after their baths. There was sweet water to drink and many kinds of food to eat.

The band of travelers bathed and ate that night, and slept in silken tents. But their leader stayed and talked by the fire with the old man who tended the oasis.

"How is it that you are here? How did you come to keep this place for travelers?" asked the leader.

The old man spoke.

"Many, many years ago, I was a pilgrim as you are. Like you, I crossed the mountains and the scrub and the desert. But this oasis was merely a place to stop for water, and our group was full of despair at the journey.

"I was a young man then, younger than you are now. But I went to the leader of our people and asked if we could rest here for a while until we found new heart to go on.

"He did not want to rest long, for he was driven to

reach the far hills. He left the oasis in the morning, with only a few of our company.

"Most of us stayed here for several days to regain our strength and will. But even as we prepared to continue on our way, more travelers came to the oasis. When they saw how rested we were, they, too, decided to stay and regain their strength. Sending the rest of my group on, I stayed to welcome the newcomers.

"Then as they, in turn, prepared to leave, their leader told me that his group had almost lost heart until they had found this resting place. Because I was here to welcome them, his people were filled with new life and hope.

"He left a tent for me and seeds from the fruit which he had brought with him on the journey."

As the old man finished his long speech, the leader of the new group sat thoughtfully. "But haven't you wanted to leave and go on to the land beyond the golden hills?" he asked finally.

"Every day. But every day there is someone who needs a welcome and a place to rest. I once wanted more than anything to reach the land beyond the hills. But it came to mean more to me that the travelers were refreshed and strengthened for their journey."

The old man smiled and continued. "I know that someday someone will come who will take on the task of welcoming the travelers. Then I will be free to go to the land beyond the hills."

The leader of the group bade the old man good night and went into his tent. Behind his own tent, the old man banked the fire for the night, and sat looking toward the west, where the sun had set beyond the golden hills.

The group rested for many days at the refuge the old man had made in the desert. At last, refreshed and renewed, they gathered their belongings. Their leader stood in their midst and spoke.

"I am not going on with you. I have come to see that my task is to welcome the travelers. I have led you through the worst of the way, and the path is clear before you now.

"I ask that you take the old man who has kept this sanctuary with you on your way. And when you reach the golden land, tell them I will come as soon as someone comes to keep the oasis in my place."

The old man clasped the leader in his arms.

"You have given me a gift beyond measure. I will surely wait for your arrival when we reach the land beyond the hills."

The group said their tearful farewells to their former leader. He watched them journey away from him until they were no more than tiny specks on the horizon.

As he turned back to the tents of the oasis, he saw a few people standing on the far rise. He hurried to greet them and to bring them to the oasis, where the water was cool and sweet and the silken tents rustled in the breeze.

The Old Man

It was winter in a small town by the edge of the sea. The wind was fierce and bitter, swirling particles of ice like small bullets into the exposed face of the old man. He had come from his hourly round of the alleys and doorways of the area and now stood in the doorway of a mission stomping the snow off his boots. Above his head, a dimly lit sign proclaimed

GEORGE STREET MISSION
ALWAYS OPEN
HOT MEALS

Finally the old man turned back inside, and closed the door on the storm.

Inside was warmer than outside, although not warm enough to sit without a wrap. The air was smoky from the fireplace. It smelled of coffee, soup, sweat, and dust.

The old man unbuttoned his coat and unwrapped the ancient scarf from his face. The priest washing the tables looked up at him.

"Any?" he asked of the old man.

"It's hard to tell, but I didn't see anyone. The snow makes it hard to see, though. The sign is lit, and at least the light is visible." The old man poured himself some coffee and sat at the table the priest had just cleaned.

"How many tonight?" the priest asked.

"Full house. Twenty women, seven children, forty men, fifty if you count the regulars," the old man answered, gesturing with his head at the men playing cards in the corner by the fireplace.

With a sigh the priest also poured himself a cup of coffee and joined him. After a silence, the priest spoke.

"How long have you been working here?" he asked.

For a while, the old man seemed lost in thought. "Twenty-five years, now," he said. "Every day for twenty-five years."

The priest smiled in amazement. "No vacations? No days off?"

"No, I've never wanted any." The old man looked around at the faded and dirty walls, at the long trestle tables covered with oil-cloth, at the shabby armchairs and couches near the fireplace.

"This is my home and my family. I haven't wanted to be anywhere else."

"Surely you have family or friends somewhere else?" the priest went on. But the old man did not answer.

His coffee cup empty, the old man got up wearily and took it into the kitchen. The priest followed him. He watched the old man start cutting up vegetables for another pot of soup. The priest took a pot from its hanging rack and began filling it with water. Their silence spoke of the companionship of shared tasks.

After the soup was set to cook on the stove, the old man started washing the never-ending pile of bowls and cups. The young priest took a towel and dried the dishes in silence. The men in the next room piled more wood on the fire and dealt another round of cards. Outside the wind blew harder. The curtains shivered in the drafts around the old windows.

"So how do you like serving the poor this way?" the old man asked the priest, breaking the silence at last.

The young man smiled. "When the Bishop assigned me to be curate to the church next door, he did say that part of my assignment was to be your assistant. To be honest, I rather dreaded it. But so far—"

"So far it's been kitchen duty, not care of souls?" The old man smiled at him. "Stomachs need to be fed as well as souls, my friend."

"How did you end up here?" the priest asked. "If you want to tell me, that is?"

The old man smiled. "I didn't end up here. I started here. I bought this building 25 years ago and began this mission."

The priest looked startled. "I'm sorry," he began, "I thought you—"

"I know, you thought I was one of the guests. It's all right. Had life been different I could be one of them."

The old man looked over at the handful of men at the fireplace. "Sometimes life doesn't turn out the way you expect it to, and you find yourself sleeping in a chair at the mission instead of earning a living and having a home to go to."

The dishes finished, the two poured themselves more coffee and went back to sit at the table.

"You asked if I had family," the old man said. "Long ago, I was married to the most beautiful woman you ever saw. She was kind and gentle, and I thought the sun rose in her eyes. We had a daughter, another beauty like her mother, but without her gentleness.

"I was young then, and thought I knew everything about children. I thought that it was important to control children, and to make sure they did what they were told. Perhaps if my wife had lived longer, things would have been different, but she died when our daughter was only 10."

The old man drank from his coffee cup. "After that, somehow my daughter and I never were able to speak without anger. There was nothing at all we agreed on. One day she left saying she was getting married. After that—" his voice trailed off.

"Did you ever see her again?" the priest asked after a pause.

"Once, maybe two years later. She came home with her baby saying she left her husband." The old man's faded eyes clouded with tears.

"I told her to get out, that she chose him over me, and she had to live with her choice." His voice was so soft it was barely audible. "I never saw her again."

"But didn't you ever look for her?" the priest asked.

The old man did not answer. After a long pause, he looked up again. "What? I didn't hear your question."

"I asked if you ever looked for her?" the priest repeated.

"I have never stopped looking for her. But I never even knew the name of the man she married, or where he was from. I never even asked her the name of her baby, my grandson.

"I didn't start this mission because this town needed one, you know. I wouldn't have you think I am just some saintly old man who spread goodness among the poor, because I am not. I started this mission because 25 years ago there was no place for my daughter, or anyone's child, to run to.

"All these years I have hoped and waited for someone to come in who knows her, who knows what became of her. That's why I never dare to take time away from here. I am afraid if I do I will miss her or someone who knows her. Perhaps you've seen her? Here, let me show you her picture."

The old man pulled a much creased envelope from his pocket and reverently slid a photograph from it. The picture was faded, showing a pretty girl of 20 smiling mischievously into the camera.

The priest took the picture and stared at it.

"It is an old picture, I know. But it is the only one I have of her." The old man's voice was soft.

After a long pause, the priest looked up to meet the old man's eyes. "I'm very sorry, but, no, I don't believe I have ever seen her," he said apologetically.

"I know. In any case, the picture is so old. She's probably a grandmother herself by now."

Outside the wind seemed to be dying down a bit. The cardplayers were preparing to sleep in the shabby chairs by the fire.

With a long sigh, the old man put the precious photograph back into its envelope, and gently put the envelope back into his shirt pocket. Then he stood up and began to button his heavy coat once again. The priest watched as he wrapped the scarf around his face, leaving only his eyes showing.

"It's time to check the alleys again," the old man said through the scarf. "You will be here for a while?"

The priest nodded. The old man slid the door open carefully, letting in only a little of the winter's storm.

"God go with you," the priest said to the old man's back.

The Potter's Gift

any years ago, in a small village, there lived a potter. This potter was a wonderful craftsman who made all kinds of things from the natural gray-brown clay dug from the riverbank that ran by the village.

The potter made the cups and plates and bowls of the villagers' daily life, the great baptismal bowl for the village church, toys for the children, and humble bowls for their animals.

But of all the things he made, none was more beautiful than his vases. Each vase would take him several weeks, even months to create. ~~Each was a wonder to see~~. They were truly the work not only of great skill, but of great faith and love. For each vase was almost alive in color and form, wondrous in golden yellow, or green-blue like the river in summer.

After he finished each new vase, the potter would call in his friends. The whole village would rejoice at the beauty of his creation.

The potter never sold these vases but gave them as gifts to his friends and neighbors. After many years, nearly every home in the village, and many homes in the surrounding villages, were graced by these lovely creations.

Each home where his vases stood seemed a little brighter, a little warmer, touched with the scent of the flowers that always filled the vases.

But there was one home in the village that had no vase. This was the home of the potter's neighbor, the schoolmaster. Never were two men more unalike. The potter, in all his years, had never traveled beyond the surrounding villages. The schoolmaster, had traveled through many lands in his youth. The schoolmaster spoke and wrote in many foreign tongues; the potter could not even read in his own tongue.

There was no home closed to the potter; none seemed open to the schoolmaster. Although the villagers had often invited him to share in their hospitality when he had first arrived, he had always refused. Now the schoolmaster neither accepted nor extended invitations.

But perhaps the greatest difference between the two men was this. The potter rose each day with a smile on his ancient, lined face, eager to welcome the new day. The schoolmaster dreaded each day, and taught his lessons with a ferocious and inflexible will.

Each year the heart of the schoolmaster grew harder and colder. Each year his soul grew narrower and darker. Even his small cottage seemed to grow smaller and darker with each passing year. The sun at noon did not penetrate far into the heavily curtained windows of his house.

If the sun could have reached past the schoolmaster's guarded windows, it would have shined on the barest essentials of life—a table and chair, a bookcase jammed with papers and books, an old wardrobe, and the narrowest of beds. No pictures decorated the walls; no rugs softened the chill of the floor.

One day, as the schoolmaster was sitting to eat his solitary evening meal, there was a knock at the door. When the schoolmaster answered, he was amazed to see the potter standing at his door, holding a heart-of-fire red vase in his hands.

"I have come to bring you this gift," said the potter, "May I come in?"

The schoolmaster, in amazement, stepped back to let him in.

The potter put the magnificent vase on the table, where its glowing beauty contrasted with the dark chill of the room.

"Why have you brought this?" the schoolmaster asked suspiciously. "I have no need for such gaudy trinkets, and less need for the flowers they hold."

"I know," said the potter gently. "That is why I brought it."

"I do not understand you. I say I have no use for a thing and you say that is why you give it. Take it back with you!" the schoolmaster said harshly.

"I cannot do that. It was made for you and it cannot belong to anyone else. But I will tell you this: someday you will see the flowers this vase was made to hold. And when you do, you will know why I brought it." With that, the potter smiled and left the schoolmaster still gazing angrily at the vase.

For days the vase sat on the table. Each time the schoolmaster saw it, he was filled with anger at the potter who gave him something so utterly useless. Yet its beauty was too great to allow the schoolmaster to break it.

After a while, the schoolmaster put the vase on a shelf. It sat next to his old worn books and the uncorrected compositions of the schoolmaster's few students.

The vase grew dim on the shelf. Dust and neglect soon covered its glowing beauty. From time to time the schoolmaster would catch sight of its lovely shape, now covered with cobwebs and dust, and he would grow angry again at the potter.

One day, as the schoolmaster was reaching for an old book, his sleeve caught the vase. It fell and broke into a hundred pieces.

The schoolmaster gathered the fragments, which still held a little of its heart-of-fire red. Something almost like grief swept over him, but the schoolmaster shook it aside.

"Now I no longer have to worry about this stupid gift," he thought aloud, but his voice was not as steady as it usually was.

It wasn't long after that day that the schoolmaster happened to be walking home at the end of another tiring day. He was angry with the few students who came to school, for none seemed to know or care about the things the schoolmaster knew.

He was angrier still at the many students who no longer came to school, for they had figured out ways to avoid the very thing the schoolmaster himself could not avoid.

That day his feet seemed reluctant to go back to his gloomy cottage. He found himself walking down the old worn path that ran by the river. As he looked at the calm gray-green of the river flowing past the old mill, his eyes were caught by a flash. Something that glowed red was growing by the crumbling stone of the old mill wall.

There, in the midst of the broken stone, were three wild lilies, all in shades of heart-of-fire red. They were so like his vase in color and form that there was no doubt these were the flowers the vase was made to hold.

But as the schoolmaster went to pick the lilies, he remembered with a ~~sudden searing~~ flash of pain that the vase was destroyed.

For the first time since he had been a child, the schoolmaster felt ~~the warmth of~~ tears trickle down his cheeks. With a ~~wild~~ despairing face, the schoolmaster ran to the potter.

"You must make me a new vase. Mine is broken, and I have found the flowers that were meant for it." ~~With a harsh rattle~~, his voice broke.

For what seemed like eternity, the potter did not speak. At last, he shook his head sadly. "I cannot do that, for it takes weeks to make a vase, and each one is the only one of its kind. Even if I were to make another one in the same hue and shape, it would not be the same at all. I am very sorry."

The schoolmaster covered his face with his hands

with a despairing cry and sank to his knees on the floor. Then he wept the tears of a broken child.

"I am sorry—please forgive me—I counted your gift as something useless, valueless. Now I see what it was—forgive me," the schoolmaster choked out the words from his tormented soul.

The potter leaned down and placed his hand on the schoolmaster's shoulder. "My friend, do not despair. It is true that I cannot give you another vase like the red one that was lost. But I will give you another I was saving."

The potter went to the end of the cottage, where he had his kiln and his wheel. In a moment he returned with a vase gloriously golden yellow, a vase that seemed to shine as the sun.

"Here, my friend, have this one." The potter smiled as he put the vase in the trembling hands of the schoolmaster.

The schoolmaster cradled the gift in his arms as a mother holds her infant. The tears that fell unheeded from his eyes seemed only to make the vase glow more golden.

All the languages he knew, all the knowledge he took pride in, turned unimportant as the schoolmaster contemplated the potter's gift. At last he turned his eyes to the potter and said simply, "Thank you."

From that moment the schoolmaster was like a man who had recovered from a deadly illness. The change began when he drew back the curtains in his front window to put the vase on the sill of his window in a space of honor. When he saw how dark the windows had become with dirt and neglect, he spent the rest of the day taking down the old worn curtains and cleaning the windows.

Once placed in the newly shined window, the magnificence of the vase radiated light into the far corners of the schoolmaster's dark cottage. Seeing how cold and cramped his house had become, he spent the next few days cleaning and polishing the inside of his house.

Several days after he had received the gift of the vase, there was a knock. When he opened the door, he found several children from the village standing on his doorstep. These were the children he had been trying to teach for years, the children who would cross the street rather than speak to him. Now they stood at his door, unsure of their welcome, their arms full of glorious yellow and white daisies.

For a moment the schoolmaster and the children eyed each other with caution. Then a smile, slow, yet with the light of the golden vase, spread over the schoolmaster's face. No child had smiled before in his presence, but now each smiled in response.

"We heard you wanted some flowers for your vase," they said, as they poured out their gift on his table. Their eyes darted about the room.

"You do not have many things at all, do you?" asked one little girl.

He looked at his house with her eyes. He saw the emptiness not only of the cottage but also of the life it represented.

He nodded and sighed. Then he smiled at the children again.

"It doesn't matter," he assured them. "After all, we have flowers for the vase."

After the children had gone, the schoolmaster arranged the daisies in the wondrous golden vase. The presence of the flowers did, indeed, make up for what the room lacked.

The next day, as the schoolmaster was preparing to paint the walls of his tiny cottage, again there came a knock on the door. When he opened it, he saw to his amazement two men from the carpenter's shop carrying two beautifully carved armchairs.

"These are yours," the men said, as they placed them on each side of his small fireplace.

"But I did not order any chairs!" he answered in surprise.

"We were told to deliver them to you." The carpenter replied.

"But who—why?" The schoolmaster could not finish.

"We can't tell you that. Only that they're a gift." The men shrugged. "Good morning to you."

After the two men left, the schoolmaster stared in wonder at the chairs. Truly they were beautifully carved, with arms and back as smooth as silk. On each seat was a tapestry of daisies and other flowers of the field, each in a vase that was surely copied from his own.

As he sat bewildered, someone called from the doorway behind him.

"The door was open," said a smiling, plump woman in the doorway. "I heard you needed curtains."

As he took the bundle of folded cloth from her hands and held it up, he nearly exclaimed aloud. The fabric was of shades of white and yellow, seemingly shot through with threads of gold. He hung them in his front window. They framed the vase with such perfection it seemed they had always been there.

When he turned to thank the woman, she was gone.

In the days and weeks that followed, it seemed to the schoolmaster that the entire village came to his door on one errand or another.

Neighbors brought gifts of preserves and bread, gifts of paintings for his bare walls, of quilts for his meager bed. When the daisies in the vase began to fade, the village children brought him armfuls of yarrow, Queen Anne's lace, and golden daylilies.

After he had the vase for a month and realized what the potter's gift had come to mean in his life, the schoolmaster went back to his neighbor.

"You have given me a gift beyond measure. Because of your gift, my life has become new and wonderfully sweet. For the first time I look my neighbors in the eye and call them my friends.

"All of this has come about from the gift you gave to me. Is there anything I can give in return?"

The potter meditated, then spoke. "I have no children of my own to carry on my shop when I am dead. If you are willing to become my student, I will teach you to become a potter."

"Certainly. I will come as soon as the school day is over."

"No," said the potter. "I am asking you to give up being a teacher and become a potter."

The schoolmaster looked shocked. Then he slowly said, "For years I have taken pride in my knowledge and my gifts of language. I have been a teacher as long as I have been an adult. But your gift of creation and beauty surpasses the greatest knowledge I have ever learned. If you will have me, I will spend my life becoming a potter like you."

And so it was that the proud schoolmaster became in his prime the humble apprentice to the potter. At first, he only made the rough bowls for the villagers' pets, the cups and plates for their daily tables. But in time, he learned the wonder of the vases' creation, and how to make them be the heart-of-fire red, the evening blue, the wondrous yellow-gold.

The former schoolmaster's house was now always filled with the laughter of children and the warmth of friends. The homes of the villagers were open to him.

Each home had two vases now, one from the old potter and one from the new. And the village rejoiced in the beauty and joy that the vases brought to them.

But only one vase stood in the window of the former schoolmaster, for it was to him the greatest gift, the sign of life made new.

The Iron Gate

The great stone mansion was surrounded at a distance by an even greater stone wall. The wall stood much higher than the tallest man, and its outer edge was smooth and gave no hand or foot hold. No trees or even vines grew near the wall to let anyone climb over.

Why the wall had been built around the great mansion, no one was quite sure. Some people told their children that long ago the wall had kept out the legions of armed men that preyed on the countryside. Others just as firmly believed that the wall was meant to keep the followers of some long-dead ruler secluded from the harsh life outside the wall.

Whatever the reason, the wall now surrounded a village that had grown up around the central mansion. The village was sheltered from both natural and human trouble, and the people lived in peace and security.

The only way through the wall was a formidable iron gate, hung on massive hinges bolted to the stone wall. Many people came from far away to stand at the gate. They waited there because occasionally, by some schedule known only to those who lived within the wall, the gate would open. Then those who were at the gate were welcomed in to the village.

Sometimes when the gate opened, there were only a few waiting to enter. Other times so many waited at the gate that latecomers feared being turned away. But no one had ever been denied entrance, although the wait was often very long.

One day the nobleman who lived in the great house in the center of the village was at breakfast. The captain of his guards was admitted.

"I'm sorry to disturb you, sir, but it's about the people again," the captain began apologetically. "The people at the gate."

The nobleman raised his eyebrows. "I thought I gave orders to admit them today."

"Yes, sir, you did. That is, we did." The captain started again. "We did admit them, sir, except there is one who will not come in. Should we close the gate on her or leave it open?"

"Why won't she come in?" the lord was puzzled.

"I don't know, sir. All she says is that she can't come in because she promised to wait," the captain said.

"Wait for what?" the lord asked. A frown creased his face.

"She does not say, sir. But she is standing in the path of the gate and will not leave. We could remove her but we were not sure what you wanted us to do." The guardsman stood at attention.

The lord wiped his lips carefully with his napkin. "I think I should go and talk to her myself."

The guardsman accompanied the nobleman to the

gate. As they passed through the village, they could hear the sounds of celebration as the newcomers were welcomed.

When the captain and the nobleman approached the gate, they could see the small figure of a young girl leaning against the stone edge of the gateway. She was covered with dust from the road. She seemed terribly thin and tired. The stone she leaned against towered far over her head, and the massive iron gate dwarfed her.

The girl turned to face the two men as they approached.

"Why won't you let my man close the gate?" the nobleman began.

"I promised I'd wait for someone," she answered in a gentle voice.

"Come inside and wait here," the nobleman went on, impatience edging his voice.

"Yes, come inside. There is food and clean clothes waiting for you," the guardsman added persuasively.

The girl shook her head.

"No, for then I cannot see and help him if he needs me," she answered again in her quiet voice. She turned to look back down the path.

"Look, I'll have the guard stay with you, and when your friend comes, he'll open the gate for him." The nobleman was becoming more impatient.

She turned back to the man, her eyes brimming. "I told him I would wait for him. I told him I would make sure the gate would be open when he came. Don't you see? If he sees the gate is closed, he will turn back. He will think I didn't wait for him."

For a moment, no one spoke. Then the girl went on, tears running unchecked.

"He is my brother, but he is so slow. He cannot walk very fast, so I was angry at him and left him with some other people who were coming. I told him that he was making me late, that the gate would open and we would be too late. So I ran on ahead. But I promised him I would wait for him.

"That was many days ago. Now that I am here I. . . ." Her voice trailed off as she looked again down the roadway.

After a moment she went on. "If you need to close the gate, I understand." She moved from the gateway to the road outside. "I'm sorry I stopped your man from closing it before."

She looked back at the two men. "Well? Go ahead! Close the gate."

The nobleman shook his head as the guard went to the gate. "In all the years we have opened the gate to admit people, no one has ever done this. Are you sure you wish to wait outside the gate for your brother?"

The girl nodded, but she said nothing.

"You do realize, don't you, that you may never have another chance to come in?" the nobleman went on.

The girl nodded again.

"I hope he knows what you are giving up to wait for him," the captain of the guards added.

"It doesn't matter," the girl said softly. "If I have to

choose between your village and my brother, then I will choose him."

The nobleman stood for a moment in deep thought. Twice the captain of the guards started to say something, but the other man held up his hand in admonition.

Then, as the girl began to gather up her few belongings to return home with them, the nobleman spoke.

"Wait!" He turned to the guardsman and spoke quickly to him. The guardsman left, returning shortly with many men holding long iron poles.

The men and the nobleman then raised the great iron gate off its massive hinges. It took nearly an hour, but at last the gate crashed to the ground.

As the men returned to their work, the nobleman walked through the now empty gateway to the girl. His beautiful clothes were torn and stained from the iron gate, he had a long scratch on his cheek, and his hands were scraped and bleeding.

"It should have come down long ago," he said. "In fact, I have no idea why there is a gate here at all."

The girl looked up at him. "Your clothes are all torn—now you look like us." She seemed to find this amusing, for her face lit up with a luminous smile.

He shrugged his shoulders, then winced at the pain the gesture cost him.

"Are you going to wait with me?" the girl asked him.

While she was speaking, the nobleman's coach, pulled by six magnificent horses, came down the road from the village. It went through the gateway and down the road. Two men followed the coach, bringing a bench which they placed just outside the wall.

"You see, I am prepared to wait, and the coach will find your brother and bring him quickly." The nobleman sat down on the bench. He signaled to the girl to join him.

But she was still anxious. "Is there room in the coach for the people he is with?"

"There is room for a dozen people in it. If we need to, we can send it out again and again until they are all here."

Finally the girl seemed satisfied. She sat on the bench and turned to him. "Sir, why is there a wall around your village?"

"Until this morning, I had never thought about the wall much," he said. "It's funny. When I was young, I often asked people why there was a wall there. They always said it was there to protect us. Then they would pat me on the head and say how much we needed the wall, and that it had always been there.

"But until you came, I never realized what a wall did to those who live outside it." He went on. "I think it's time the wall came down."

"Will the people in your village like that?" The girl turned her young eyes to him.

"No. I'm sure there will be many who will not like it at all. There are many people in my village who do not like to think of themselves as being like other people. After all, they are from the village within the wall. Just the same, maybe we don't need the wall as much as we thought we did."

"But won't some of them leave? Or try to stop you?" the girl asked anxiously.

"Probably," he said a little sadly. "What about you? Will you stay even if there is no wall to hide behind?"

"Of course. Since you took down the gate for me, of course I will stay and help you take down the wall." The girl smiled up at him again, her luminous eyes aglow. "I think you'll need a lot of help."

The nobleman took her small hand in his. "I think you are right."

The Willow Flute

t was the glorious and long-awaited first day of summer. The sun shone on the sea. The turquoise water gleamed and rippled under the off-shore breeze. A young girl skipped down the sandy shore road to the cracked boardwalk and down the old wooden steps leading to the shore. At the edge of the sand she stopped and took off her sandals to let the warm sand caress her feet.

The girl continued down the shore. She passed a deserted summer cottage and a collapsed ice-fishing hut that had been dragged onto the shore the previous winter.

From time to time she stooped to pick up a pebble worn smooth by the sea or a shell that caught her fancy. She dropped them all into the pocket of her sleeveless dress, ignoring the sand and the wetness her treasures brought with them.

The tide was out, but not yet all the way. It still teased the rock sea-wall protecting the beach. Gulls squawked at each other as they discovered and ate soft sand creatures.

But the girl didn't mind the birds. When they rose in

a clatter to the sky, she laughed and waved to them, with the contentment of summer and peace.

Sensing someone approaching, she turned. She greeted the newcomer with a great wide grin of welcome.

The newcomer smiled and nodded in acknowledgment. Plump and gray-haired, she looked old to the girl. She carried a small sack out of which stuck the ends of a dozen medium sized twigs. When the woman had found a suitable rock, she sat and carefully selected a willow twice the size and length of her finger. The woman pulled a small knife from her sack and started peeling the twig.

The girl watched at a distance. Neither spoke. Finally the girl walked closer. The woman looked up.

"What are you making?" the child asked at last, her curiosity outweighing her reluctance to talk to strangers.

"Flutes," the woman answered with a smile.

"What are they?" the girl asked.

The woman looked up from the willow she had peeled. The twig was now yellow-white and shining.

"Flutes? Well, the real flutes are wonderful musical instruments, silvery and sounding like summer birds. These are flutes' poor cousins, but if they are well made, they, too make a lovely sound. Have you ever heard a flute played?" the woman asked.

"I don't think so—I don't listen to music much," the girl answered thoughtfully, a crease furrowing her young forehead.

"I could not live without music," said the woman. "If

you will fill this basin with water from the pool over there, you can see how I make them."

The girl ran with the basin to the tidal pool that the receding tide had forgotten. She filled it and returned, sloshing a good deal of the water on her dress.

The woman placed the first willow in the basin. She began to peel a second.

"Would you care to peel them, too?" the woman asked. When the girl hesitated, the woman pulled out a scraper. "You don't need a knife to peel them. The bark is soft and peels easily once you get it started."

The two sat in companionable silence, peeling the twigs. At last, they had a respectable pile soaking in the seawater.

"Now we soak them to loosen them up. This is the long part." The woman put the scraper and knife away again. She took out a thin metal rod, about half as thick as the willows. She pulled out a small hammer. Reaching into the basin, she pulled out the first willow she had peeled.

"Why can't you live without music?" the girl asked.

The woman gently tapped the metal rod into the middle of the willow. She considered the question.

"I don't know really. I guess I have been around music for so long that I need it the way you need air and sunlight." The rod had driven the middle of the first willow clear. The woman held up the hollow twig and the girl applauded.

"Now what?" the girl said. But the woman did not answer. Instead, she placed the hollowed out willow to dry on a nearby rock.

"Did you say something?" the woman turned back to the girl.

"No, that's all right. You answered me anyway," the girl replied.

"We push out the middle and then we let them all dry. When that's done, we can put holes in them so they will make lovely music for us," the woman went on.

The morning passed quickly. The sun rose higher. The tide drew back into the sea, leaving little rivulets of water coursing across exposed sand. The seabirds complained to each other as they coaxed tiny creatures from the mud.

After all the willows were hollowed out, the woman took a pointed tool and bored out eight small holes down the length of the hollowed stem. She notched a small, triangular piece out near one end.

With a smile, the woman handed the first flute to the girl.

"I don't know how to play," the girl admitted.

"Wait until I make another, then, and I'll show you how." The woman finished the second in only a minute and showed the girl how to hold her hands to make the flute play. While the girl practiced, the woman finished the pile of flutes.

As she rose to wash her hands in the water, the girl called to her, "Do they all sound alike?"

The woman did not answer. Then, when she returned to where the girl was, she noticed the hurt look.

"Did you ask me something? I'm sorry if I did not

hear you. I am deaf. I can only hear you if I can see you."

The girl felt a flush creep up her face, as though she had said a very impolite thing. But the smile on the woman's face and her gentle tone were reassuring.

"I didn't realize--" the girl began awkwardly. A puzzled look crossed her face. "If you cannot hear, why do you make these?" The girl pointed to the neat pile of flutes.

"I haven't been deaf all my life. Years ago, I was terribly sick one summer and could only lie outside in a lawn chair, under the trees. My parents taught me ways to pass the time. My mother taught me how to embroider and how to make lace, and my father showed me how to make these." The woman smiled at the girl.

"Did your father make a lot of flutes, too?" the girl asked.

"Except for the ones he made to show me, I never saw him make any. He was always busy, concerned about money and the household and all. Since he died, I come down here every now and then to make all the flutes he never found time to make.

"Then I take them up to the village. I teach the children how to make them and how to play them." The woman looked out to sea for a long time.

"But you said you could not live without music. How can that be?" The girl asked, curious. When the woman did not answer, the girl touched her arm. The woman turned her head back to the girl, who repeated her question.

"I can hear music all the time in my mind. Many times, it is easier to hear that way, because neither people, barking dogs, nor all the noise the world makes interrupt me."

Then the woman turned from her reverie and said briskly, "But come, child, the day is half gone, and I'm sure people are looking for both of us. If you come up to the village square later today, you can meet other children and learn how to make wonderful music on your flute."

The woman put the completed instruments into the bag she carried. The girl waved as the woman walked back up the long wood stairs to the old boardwalk, and on to the shore road, back the way she had come.

Already Paid For

n a small village, there was a store that sold a little bit of everything: food, cloth, nails, boots, whatever you might need. For many years, it had been run by one man. Since his death a year ago, his widow had run the store. Although she was good at this, the things her husband had done to keep the roof in repair, the lamps mended, and the windows tight, seemed beyond her.

But she struggled to deal with the repairs as best she could until she finally admitted she needed help. So she placed a notice in her front window. It said,

HANDYMAN NEEDED!
INQUIRE WITHIN.

The very next day, a stranger came into her store and told her he was a handyman. He had been passing through town and had seen her sign. Then he asked what she needed done. After she gave him her long list, she was afraid to ask what he would charge.

Seeing her hesitation, he said, "I will ask only what is fair for wages. You will be able to afford it, I assure you."

Although still nervous, she agreed.

In just a few days the man had fixed everything on her list—and a few things that weren't. The roof was whole, the windows were tight, the lamps were mended.

"What do I owe you?" she asked, feeling that even a vast sum was well worth the price.

"Nothing," the man said.

"Nothing!"

"I have already been paid for my work here," he said.

"Who paid you?"

"A friend of yours. I'm afraid I do not remember the name, but I assure you, you owe nothing." The man was firm.

"But surely you will take something—as a gift."

The man smiled.

"Yes, I could do that. I need two small lamps and a warm blanket."

The storekeeper gave him the lamps and the blanket gratefully, adding extra oil for the lamps and a pillow.

He thanked her and turned to go.

"If you know of anyone else who needs a handyman, ask them to put a note in their windows as you did." And he left.

It was then that the storekeeper realized she never asked his name.

The next day, one of the poor villagers who lived out beyond the river visited the storekeeper. The woman, bent with age, seemed uncomfortable being in the store.

"Can I help you?" the storekeeper asked.

The old woman shook her head. "I came to thank you for the lamps and the blanket."

The storekeeper was puzzled.

"I haven't given you any lamps or blankets."

"Your friend came to my door with them yesterday. He said they were a gift from you. He said I should thank you." The old woman turned to leave. Then she turned back.

"I haven't had a pillow to sleep on in many, many years. Thank you, my dear." And she walked out of the store, leaving the other woman staring at her in wonder.

When the news of the extraordinary handyman made its way through the village, many of the villagers decided that things in their homes needed repairing. Each time they placed a note in their windows, the man would come and do as they requested. It seemed as though there was nothing he could not fix, whether in the garden, in the barns and sheds, or in the kitchen.

Each time he refused payment, saying that he had already been paid in full. But each time he was willing to accept small gifts.

From the gardener he received seeds for vegetables and flowers. From the baker, he received a measure of flour. From the woodsman he received a barrow full of small logs.

The weaver gave a length of heavy woolen cloth. When he fixed the tailor's sewing machine, he asked the tailor to make a winter coat from the cloth.

A few days after the handyman had taken the coat, the weaver and the tailor were both visited by one of the poor fishermen from the dockside. The fisherman thanked them for their gift, which allowed him to take his boat out in cold weather and feed his children.

And in a few days people came and thanked the gardener and the baker and the woodsman for their gifts.

Little by little, the village changed. Once the rest of the villagers had neglected the poor people among them. Now they knew and cared for even the poorest person.

In time, all the villagers became kinder—except the doctor. The doctor had been raised in the village but had gone away to school. He had returned to the village several years ago when the previous doctor had died.

It was rumored that the doctor had suffered greatly in his life, for there was no other explanation for his grim face and angry scowl. Although he was a capable doctor, many people were afraid of him. He was often called far too late to help the sick in the village.

The doctor had an antique clock in his parlor that was one of his many objects of pride. The clock had been given to the doctor by one of his instructors at medical school. But it had not worked in years, and the doctor did not trust the village clock maker to fix it.

As always, the handyman came in response to the doctor's message.

The doctor began. "Unlike many of my neighbors, I am well able to pay you. You cannot tell me that you have already been paid by a friend, for I have no friends who would do such a thing. If you are able to fix my clock, I will pay any price."

The handyman went to the clock and looked at it for a long moment.

"I can fix this clock, but it will cost you a great deal. Are you certain that is what you want to do?"

The doctor frowned and nodded.

"It is worth any price."

The handyman smiled. "Do not be so quick to answer, my dear sir. You haven't yet heard my price."

The doctor waved his hand.

"I can afford it. I am a very wealthy man."

The handyman only smiled again. "Very well. I can begin now."

The doctor nodded abruptly and went back to see one of his few patients.

The next day, the doctor was awakened by the sound of the clock in his parlor ringing the hour. He ran to the clock and saw that the handyman had indeed fixed it.

When the handyman returned for his payment, the doctor asked, "What is your price?"

The handyman said, "Before I answer, I would like to ask you something."

The doctor nodded.

"How did you come to be a doctor?"

"I was always interested in medicine and I did very well in school. When I said I wanted a career in medicine, my mother and father agreed that it was a good choice."

The handyman interrupted. "And did they pay for your schooling?"

"Yes, of course they did. Some of the people in the

village also helped, with the condition that I would come back to the village and be their doctor for ten years. The years I promised the village are nearly up. Soon I will be free to move to the city and live as a wealthy and influential man."

After a pause, the handyman asked another question. "Did you ever pay your parents back for the sacrifices they made so you could have this education and privilege?"

The doctor smiled. "They were pleased that I wanted to spend my life in service to others and said they were willing to make any necessary sacrifices."

The handyman went on. "Did you ever thank them?"

The doctor frowned. "For what? They did not ask me to repay them. I do not owe anyone for who I am, except the villagers. I have very nearly paid that debt. Now, what do I owe you for fixing my clock?"

The handyman stood up and said sadly, "Nothing."

"I told you that I am well able to pay my debts. How much do I owe you?" the doctor responded angrily.

"You owe me nothing. I fixed your clock because it is a clock of great beauty, and things of beauty should not be silent. It will keep perfect time for you for many, many years. But because it is only a timepiece to you, it is not worth fixing. Therefore, I will not charge you."

The handyman turned to go. "It's too bad, in a way. You have the finest house, the most beautiful clock I have ever seen. Indeed, your possessions make you the envy of many poorer people. But of all the people I have met in your village, you are the most in need. You have nothing I would even ask for as a gift."

After the handyman left, the doctor stormed angrily from room to room in his lovely house. He admired the fine furnishings, the expensive paintings on each elegant wall, the imported lace curtains on each window.

As he walked through his house, he raged at the handyman. "How dare a wandering handyman, a tinker with no place to lay his head, say such things? Doesn't he know who I am?"

On the hour, his clock chimed in its lovely voice. For a moment, the doctor was tempted to smash the clock, and end its voice forever. But he could not destroy his expensive and beautiful clock.

For days after, the doctor was more grim and angry than usual. Fury at the handyman who had dared to say such things about him filled him every time the clock chimed.

A few weeks later, the doctor stood waiting for his carriage. He saw the handyman across the street. The doctor wanted to confront the handyman and demand that the man take back the things he had said. But as he stepped off the curb, a great rush of sound enveloped him.

There were loud shouts of "Runaway!" and a clatter of horses' hooves on the cobblestones. A tremendous push shoved the doctor backward onto the curbing as the immense wheels of a carriage passed close to his face. With a mighty surge of deafening noise, the runaway coach passed down the street.

As the doctor lay stunned on the stone curbing, he was aware of a new sound, that of heartbreaking sobs. The doctor pulled himself to his feet. He saw the handyman lying broken and bleeding. He had been struck by the coach and horses after he had pushed the doctor. Several townspeople were already at his side, and one was weeping bitterly.

When the doctor reached the injured man's side, he saw that the man was beyond help. The doctor knelt by his side and took one of the handyman's bloody hands in his own. For a moment the doctor thought the man was already dead, but slowly the handyman opened his dimming eyes and looked into the doctor's eyes.

"Why?" was all the doctor could murmur to the dying man.

A smile lit up the handyman's broken face. "You are my friend," he said in faint tones.

The doctor's eyes filled with tears that poured down his cheeks unnoticed. "Thank you," the doctor murmured to the dying man. With a smile still on his face, the handyman died.

The townspeople buried him in the old graveyard behind the church. They did not know his name, so the stone marker simply read, "Our Friend."

In his office, after the man's interment, the doctor was slowly packing up his equipment and books. As he had told the handyman, his ten years of service to the town was ended. A new doctor had been hired. As he looked over the last set of bills to go out to his patients, his office sign, now leaning against the wall, caught his eye. The sign read, "Doctor Within" and gave his office hours.

The doctor sat there for a long time. Finally, with a great sob, the doctor took the bills he was about to mail and wrote, "Already Paid in Full" across all of them and thrust them into their envelopes. Then he took the office sign and went outside and hung it back where it had been for ten years.

When he came back in, he drew out his pen and paper, and began to write, "Dearest Mother and Father, I can never thank you enough for your gifts of love and support that have made my life and my occupation possible. . . ."

From the parlor behind him, the doctor heard his clock chiming the hour.

Made with Love

n old woman sat in an ancient wooden rocking chair by the edge of a blackened fireplace. The fire snapped and muttered to itself in the chimney. She sat staring into the flames, rocking back and forth, back and forth. She seemed ages old, far older than her real years, worn and frail as ancient paper. Her face was angular and the end-of-day shadows left great dark smudges under her eyes and on her thin cheeks. She rested one hand on the battered cane that was her constant companion. Back and forth she rocked.

At last she sighed a great long sigh, like the sound of mighty evergreens in a cold wind. She tapped her cane loudly on the floor to summon her daughter-in-law, who shared the old woman's home.

"Yes, Mama. What is it?" the younger woman came from the kitchen, wiping her hands on her apron. Her tone barely concealed her irritation at the interruption.

"Where is my shawl?" the old woman whined.

"Which one?" Her daughter-in-law made no attempt to hide her anger at the foolish question.

"The old one. The one my mother gave to me." The

irritation in the old woman's voice echoed the younger woman's tone.

"I haven't seen it in years. Why do you want that old one? It's probably long fallen into pieces. And it never was very warm. I'll get you another shawl."

Her daughter-in-law pulled a fluffy shawl from the closet and wrapped it around the old woman as though she were an ancient doll to be dressed at will.

"I wasn't cold!" The old woman flung off the shawl.

"If you're not cold, what do you need a shawl for?" The younger woman looked at the clock, as though she was late for an appointment.

"I just do! And I want you to go into the attic and look for my shawl in the old chest. I'm sure I put it there years ago." The old woman's tone was stubborn.

Her temper rising, the younger woman protested. "I really have better things to do than to go looking in a drafty cold attic for something you may have put up there years ago!"

The old woman responded in quick fury.

"I'll remind you whose house this is! Even if you are my son's widow, I didn't have to invite you to live here!"

The old woman's face was turning paler and more angular by the moment.

For a long time, the two women glared at each other, enemies in battle. Finally, the younger woman flung up her hands in angry surrender.

"Fine! I'll go and look in the attic if it's so important to you! But if your dinner is late, I don't want to hear a word out of you!"

She stomped from the room. Her wooden-heeled shoes made loud, angry steps down the hall, up the stairs, and across the attic floor.

The old woman waited in her rocker by the fire, rocking back and forth. At last, she heard footsteps returning.

"There!" shouted the younger woman as she threw the shawl at the old woman. "Now, am I allowed to get on with dinner, or is there something else you must have?"

But the older woman was silent, her attention fixed on the ancient shawl in her hands.

With a sniff of impatience, her daughter-in-law wheeled about and went back to the kitchen.

The old woman was still absorbed in the shawl when her granddaughter came to tell her supper was ready.

"Nana, what's that? It looks very old."

The child stood beside the rocker and held out her hand to caress the shawl.

For a moment, her grandmother lifted up a hand to stop the child from touching it. But the older woman held her hand, and the little girl rubbed the shawl's fringe.

"It is very old, child. My grandmother gave it to my mother, and she gave it to me. But it's even older than my grandmother, or so my mother told me."

The fabric was so brittle with age it seemed that the slightest touch might cause the shawl to dissolve into dust. It was faded brown, the color of oak leaves in winter, withered and dead.

"Come on, Nana, it's time for dinner." The child held out her arm to the old woman.

The old woman pulled herself slowly from her chair. With one hand, she supported herself on her cane. The other hand still held the shawl.

Dinner was a silent meal.

Afterward, the old woman and her granddaughter went back to the seat by the fire. As the girl turned to go, the old woman stopped her.

"Stay awhile, child." Her old voice was unusually gentle and pleading.

The girl drew up a stool and sat next to the old woman. The old woman began to speak in a soft, dreamlike voice.

"When my mother gave me this shawl, it was the loveliest thing I had ever seen. It was the softest rose-pink edged with a fringe the color of new milk. To me, it always looked like a rose dusted with snow. It was so beautiful, then." The old woman's face softened.

"When did she give it to you, Nana?" The child knew only that her great-grandmother had died when her grandmother was a child.

Her grandmother seemed lost in memories. For a long time she did not speak.

"When I was a little girl, younger than you are now, we lived in a lovely house, Papa, Mama and I. Our town was filled with the nicest, kindest people I have ever known. On summer nights, we would walk together through the town, and Mama would always wear this shawl. She said that it had been made with such love that she would never be alone when she wore it, for the love made in the shawl would always be like the welcoming arms of friends and family."

The old woman was silent for a long time.

"What happened?" the child asked her. The little girl had never heard her grandmother speak about her childhood.

"War," her grandmother said simply. "Our town was on the edge of a great forest. Soldiers came from the other side of the forest. All the young men from the village went out to fight them, but there were too many soldiers, and all the young men died.

"The soldiers set fire to the town, and we were pushed into wagons and taken far away. All the children were put in one wagon, and Mama and Papa and all the other people were put in another. When Mama said good-bye to me, she wrapped me in this shawl and kissed me. She told me never to forget that the shawl was made with love long ago, and that nothing could end that love. I never saw them again."

Her voice was almost a whisper as she finished. Her old eyes clouded with tears, but none touched her cheeks. It was as though she had used up all her tears long ago.

"Oh, Nana, how sad you must have been!" Her granddaughter's voice trembled. The tears the old woman could not shed filled her young eyes and spilled down her young cheeks, dropping onto the shawl in her grandmother's lap.

"What happened after that?" the child asked.

"After that? We were sent to a school in the town where the soldiers took us. I stayed at the school until I was old enough to work. I became a teacher in a distant village. I met your grandfather there, and we married. We came here to this village when your Papa was little."

"Did you ever go back to the town?" the child asked her.

"Once, many years later. I traveled to the place where my town had been. It had been rebuilt, but there was no one there I knew. It was full of people who moved there after the war was over. Except for some of the children who were in the school with me, there is no one who remembers the way it was then. Most of them are dead now, too."

With a great sigh, the old woman rubbed the shawl in her hands.

"Nana, look! Your shawl is turning pink." Where the old woman's hands and the child's tears touched the shawl, the dull brown color was indeed changing. In a few places, a faint pink color seemed to emerge from the brown.

"If only you could have seen it then, child. For years, I never went anywhere without it. After your grandfather died, I never seemed to wear it anymore.

"When your papa died, I thought I would die, too. But here I am, five years later, still alive." The pain in her voice was so great that her granddaughter reached out and took her hand and held it to her young cheek.

"Oh, Nana. Please do not feel sad. I love you." Again her young tears fell on the shawl in her grandmother's lap.

The old woman drew the child into her arms. For a

long time they sat together, rocking gently beside the fire.

Finally her grandmother spoke.

"It would make me very happy for you to have the shawl after I die. I know it's very old, and probably won't even outlast me. But I would like you to have it."

"I would like that, Nana," the little girl said.

But as the old woman drew the shawl around the child's shoulders, it held more than a hint of its old color. The fringe was faintly cream, and the body was the color of a faded rose. Even as the old woman's hands caressed the shawl on the child, the colors glowed more deeply, and it grew softer and warmer in her hands.

"My mother used to tell me that the love made in the shawl was so powerful nothing could destroy it. I never knew what she meant." The old woman seemed to speak to herself.

"She would tell me that as long as I wore it in love, I would always be wrapped in the arms of love." The old woman drew the child close to her again, and told her many stories about her papa when he was a little boy.

When her daughter-in-law came from the kitchen, the little girl ran to her and hugged her.

"Nana's been telling me about Papa when he was little," her daughter said.

"Won't you come and sit with us?" The old woman's voice was gentle.

The little girl's mother did not speak. She seemed to be lost in her own memories as she looked into the fire and stroked her daughter's hair.

The old woman held out her hand to her daughter-in-law.

"I know it hasn't been easy on you living here. I am sorry for the way I've treated you. I am glad you came to live with me." Tears rolled down. The younger woman took the old woman's outstretched hand.

"I'm sorry I haven't been kinder to you. I am glad we came to live here, too, Mama." She brought the other chair to the fire, and sat with her daughter in her lap.

"Tell me about your son, please. I only knew him for a short time, and there was so much we never found time to say to each other."

So the three of them started ending each day gathered at the fireside in winter or in the garden in summer, listening to the old woman tell stories of love and long ago.

Their home became a refuge and a place of comfort and love, not only for them, but for many of their friends and neighbors.

When the old woman died, she was buried between her husband and son. Her granddaughter wore the old woman's shawl and everyone who saw it was amazed at its rose and cream beauty.

Years later the old woman's granddaughter told her own daughter about the shawl, and how it had been made in love long, long ago. And the old woman's granddaughter's daughter told her children the stories of love and long ago, and she too wore the shawl in love and peace all the days of her life.

The Author

Anne L. Squire-Buresh is a native New Englander with family roots in Vermont. She is a graduate of the University of Vermont and Andover-Newton Theological School. She is also an ordained minister in the United Church of Christ.

Ms. Squire-Buresh brings a variety of work experiences to bear on her writing, including ten years of stage work, with several seasons at the Champlain Shakespeare Festival in Burlington. In addition, she has spent the last ten years working with teachers and young people in the area of religious education.

Ms. Squire-Buresh presently lives in Millbury, Massachusetts, with her husband, Donald Buresh, and two children, Emily and David. She works in the Worcester area and is active in the life of the Millbury Federated Church, particularly in the areas of education and missions. She often preaches in the Worcester area and is glad for the opportunity to give children's messages during the worship services.

Ms. Squire-Buresh has many interests, including good mystery stories, sacred music, calligraphy, and gardening. She has a long-standing interest in the art of storytelling and, in particular, the use of fables and parables to convey universal experiences.